Faster Than Fast!

𝔇ISNEY PRESS
New York • Los Angeles

Lightning races a red car.
Lightning is faster than fast!

© Disney•Pixar

Lightning races a green car.
Lightning is faster than fast!

Lightning races a yellow car.
Lightning is faster than fast!

Lightning races a white car.
Lightning is faster than fast!

Lightning races a blue car.
Lightning is faster than fast!

Lightning races a brown car.
Lightning is faster than fast!

Ka-chow!